The Night Heroes:

I0598876

Ghost

Ship

Dr. Bo Wagner

Word of His Mouth Publishers
Mooresboro, NC

All Scripture quotations are taken from the **King James Version** of the Bible.

ISBN: 978-1-941039-97-7
Printed in the United States of America
© 2015 Dr. Bo Wagner (Robert Arthur Wagner)

Word of His Mouth Publishers
Mooresboro, NC
www.wordofhismouth.com

The Night Heroes:

Ghost Ship

Chapter One

One of the greatest things about the American South is the fact that in the morning you can be in the lovely, fir-covered mountains and by that afternoon your toes can be wiggling in the sand as the saltwater of the Atlantic washes up over your feet. That thought was happily filling my mind at the moment as we made our way into the tiny town of Supply, North Carolina. At 9:00 A.M. we left Rogersville, Tennessee. Eight hours later, including stops, we were at the coast.

That is a lot of driving, but when my dad is at the wheel, the road is a giant loud-mouthed Philistine that needs a rock whopped upside its head.

Mom, who would follow my dad to the ends of the earth and back, is our best ally on days like this. If it were not for her, dad would mount a porta-potty on the back of our vehicle so we would not have to stop at all.

My two sisters and I just roll with it. When you are evangelist's kids, you have to be flexible. More than that, when you have been in a battle in the coal mines of West Virginia, jumped out of an airplane in World War II, kept two brothers from killing each other in the Civil War, and been in a knife fight with an Indian in 1788, you learn to adjust to whatever a day may bring.

No, I am not crazy, nor am I daydreaming. I am Kyle Warner, age fourteen, and along with my two sisters, Carrie, twelve, and Aly, eleven, we are the Night Heroes.

Several months ago, we were awakened in the night by a call from the Conductor. The Lord used him to send us on a mission to rescue a boy trapped by some bad men in a coal mine. We would be awake in our time during the day, then when we went to sleep, we would wake up in the past.

We would try during the time we were awake in the past to get the job done, and then at night when we went to sleep, providing we were not being held captive somewhere, we would wake back up in our time and feel just as rested as if we had gotten a full night's sleep. We had five days, and five days only, to do the job. We also learned that if we were injured in any way, we would wake up with that injury. And we discovered that whatever we went to sleep with, we carried with us into the past. That was very helpful!

Each successive mission has taught us a bit more about what is allowed and what capabilities we have. I am pretty sure our parents do not have any idea about our adventures, but sometimes I think they might. Either way, we know that each time we go to a new place there is the possibility that we will be called to another mission. Some weeks we are; some weeks we are not. Either way, we are ready.

"Are we there yet?"

That was the standard and expected question from blonde-haired Aly, the youngest member of our family and of the team. She asks it on average of once every fifteen minutes. She has energy to burn, very little patience, mood swings like a rabid pendulum, and a heart as big as Texas.

"Sure thing, honey-bunny, just tuck and roll."

That was my dad's semi-sarcastic and standard answer. We were going thirty-five miles an hour at the time.

"What will you do if she ever takes you up on that, Dad? North Carolina General Statute number 14-316.1. says 'Any person who is at least sixteen years old who knowingly or willfully causes, encourages, or aids any juvenile within the jurisdiction of the court to be in a place or condition, or to commit an act whereby the juvenile could be adjudicated delinquent, undisciplined, abused, or neglected as defined by G.S. 7B-101 and G.S. 7B-1501 shall be guilty of a Class 1 misdemeanor.' You could end up preaching your next meeting behind bars!"

That would be Carrie, my oldest sister, the braniac of our team. She is the second smartest person I know. Too bad for her, my dad is actually the smartest person I know.

"A Class 1 misdemeanor carries a maximum penalty of one hundred twenty days in jail and a discretionary fine. One hundred twenty days of peace and quiet might be worth not having to be asked that same question every fifteen minutes, and I have enough money from the last love offering to pay the fine."

Good one, dad, good one!

Carrie and Aly did not seem to think so, both of them actually "harumphed!" in unison.

Mom rolled her eyes.

I laughed.

Then the girls "harumphed" at me.

Yep, never a dull moment in this family, waking or sleeping.

We drove to just outside of Supply and stopped at the Econo Lodge in Shallotte. It used to be a Microtel, and it is really nice. We have stayed there many times, since there are some other good churches my dad preaches for in the area, like Sonrise Baptist which is pastored by Rodney Cox.

Dad whipped into the parking lot, and mom went to check us in. I grabbed a luggage cart and brought it out. Like a finely tuned people machine we unloaded the vehicle, loaded the cart, dad parked, we all got into room 111, and took a nice break after a day of hard driving.

The break lasted all of about fifteen minutes, which, thankfully, was about ten minutes longer than dad usually allowed us.

"Ok, people, time to pick them up and put them down. We need to be out the door and headed for church in thirty minutes. Hustle!"

Ironing, taking turns in the bathroom dressing, brushing hair and teeth, shining shoes, tying ties, spraying perfume, the entire room was a bustling beehive of activity. I always doubted that it all could be done in time, but somehow it always was, and this time was no different. Right on time we were out the door and back into the Yukon. Great vehicle, that one, 320,000 miles and counting!

It took us about ten minutes to get to the Victory Baptist Church. It is technically in Varnamtown, but everyone regards it as being in Supply. It is pastored by a wonderful, older gentleman named Leroy Martin. Pastor Martin is quiet, kind, just an absolute gem of a man. He has been faithfully shepherding that flock for twenty years or so. The church is mid-sized, pretty, and the folks are down to earth.

We had been here before, so we had some friends to catch up with. We laughed and joked and talked, but very soon it was time to begin service.

There is nothing formal about Pastor Martin. He handles the service in as laid-back of a manner as Andy Taylor handled his Sheriff's duties on the Andy Griffith show.

The service was great, people sang every song from the heart, and soon it was the best time, the preaching time.

Dad preached out of 2 Kings 5 on the dirt altar of Naaman. That is a really cool thing to think of. Naaman took dirt from Israel back to his homeland of Samaria to build an altar out of. Have you ever wondered why? After all, they had plenty of dirt in Samaria! But to Naaman, even the dirt in God's country was better. That seems to be a cool way of teaching us that the worst day as a Christian is better than the best day as a lost person!

Soon the service was done, there was a good number of people at the altar thanking God during the invitation, and then the service was concluded, and we had a light supper in the fellowship hall.

We didn't stay long. Our dad and mom really are great parents, and part of being a great parent is making sure your kids get enough sleep. Man, if they only knew!

Anyway, we soon said our goodbyes for the night and made our way back to the hotel. In about twenty minutes time we were all kneeling together, praying, and hugging each other good night. Then it was mom and dad to one bed, Carrie and Aly to another, and me to my blow-up mattress on the floor. The lights were out, but my heart was still awake. I had so much to thank God for, and so, like so many nights, I lay there for a while with my eyes closed, lifting up grateful praise to the God who loves me and has given me so very much. I decided a long time ago that there is no better way to end a day than praying yourself to sleep.

Chapter Two

"AVAST THERE, MATEYS, LOOK ALIVE! HEAVE TO! HOIST THE JOLLY ROGER OR I'LL HAVE YE ALL KEEL HAULED!"

The booming pirate voice had quite an effect. Carrie, ever the protector, jumped up and instinctively looked around for Aly to make sure she was okay. Aly sat straight up and looked around, wild eyed, disoriented, but determined. I rolled up onto one knee in a defensive posture, placing myself between the voice and my sisters. Whatever this new danger was, we were instantly ready to meet it.

There was no danger, there was only laughter, a deep, booming belly laugh. It was the Conductor, who apparently, in addition to being able to pilot about any type of a vessel, could also do excellent impersonations.

The laughter finally subsided, and the three of us just shook our heads and breathed a sigh of relief.

"Good morning, Mr. Conductor, and thanks for that gentle wake up call."

"Good morning to you as well, Kyle, and also to you, Carrie and Aly."

Carrie is always pretty quick to forgive and adapt, and so, through a million watt grin, she returned in her best pirate voice, "And a hearty good mornin' to you as well, ye fine old salt, may His blessings be upon thee on this fine day!"

That brought a laugh from the Conductor himself and from me as well.

"He has a sense of humor," Aly said matter-of-factly. "Nice."

"Of course, I do, young lady; after all, it was our God who invented laughter! But I suppose it is time for us to get down to business. The good news is, we can start in a much more leisurely fashion than we did last time."

"What," Carrie grinned, "no arrows this time? What fun is that? By the way, that reminds me, how is old 'Shoot-First-Ask-Questions-Later?'"

"You are assuming I know the answer to that question. What if your assumption is incorrect?"

"And you are being evasive, just like my dad," Carrie teased.

The Conductor laughed again. I really liked this man, or angel, or whatever he is/was.

"Well, heaven forbid I should be evasive to children who have risked so much to serve and save others. I do, in fact, know the answer to your question. Obviously, in your time, Black Crow is not doing so well at all, as he is long since dead. But you clearly want to know how he is/was doing in the days since you faced off against him and his brother became chief. Black Crow is adjusting, albeit grudgingly. His brother, Falling Rain, is quickly becoming a very wise chief. Their father is declining in health and will soon die. Samuel and his father are praising God over Samuel's delivery, and soon they will have a new source of happiness in their lives. Father will be meeting a fine lady and marrying her, and she will become a wonderful second mother to Samuel.

"But now we must put aside inquiries of other times and places. Let us begin as always. Carrie, can you guess where and when you are?"

I knew that the immediate where, as in the few feet around us, would be easy for her. A blind and deaf man could very likely figure that one out.

"Well, let's begin with the obvious. We are on an old wooden ship out on the ocean. First time ever for that one!"

We were all standing by then, and Carrie did a quick scan of everything.

"The three decks of this ship tell me that it is a galleon, and that kind of ship began to be used mostly in the sixteenth century but was very much discarded by the nineteenth century. There are sailors all about the deck, and all of them have flintlock pistols carried in holsters across their chest, not down by their side. That is the kind of weapon that Edward Teach, more commonly known as Blackbeard, carried, and it is the way that he carried them. All of that tells me that we are in the early seventeen hundreds. And by your usage of phrases like 'Hoist the Jolly Roger,' I would say we are in pirate waters. The most heavily infested area of the entire world for pirates was just off the coast of North Carolina, which is not too far from where dad is preaching this week.

"Conclusion: I am guessing we are off the coast of North Carolina, probably in the Cape Fear region, sometime in the late seventeenth or early eighteenth century."

The look on the Conductor's face was so very different from anything I had ever seen in him before. It was shock; absolute, horrified shock!

"Young lady, I regret to inform you that you have made a very grave error."

Now the shocked look was on Carrie's face!

There was a pregnant pause of four or five seconds, then the Conductor broke into a grin. "This area was not normally referred to as North Carolina, nor was South Carolina normally called South Carolina in this time period. Even though they were two separate states with two separate governors, this area together was normally simply referred to as Carolina. I know that may sound like a trivial detail, but if you are to pass for authentic, every detail matters. I will give you a high A-minus, since every other detail you guessed at is meticulously, painstakingly correct.

"The year is 1724, and you are currently six miles off of the North Carolina coast."

Aly immediately rushed toward the front of the ship.

"We'll be able to see land! Out on the water the human eye can see twelve miles to the horizon!"

We all rushed up beside her, and, sure enough, she was correct. Up ahead of us was a darkening line that we knew was land. Carrie and I only looked at it for a second or two, then we both turned and stared at Aly. She apparently felt our gaze and looked from one of us to the other.

"What?"

Both Carrie and I said it at the same time, "How did you know that?"

"Hey, sometimes I read books too, ya know."

"Yeah, but, *Green Eggs and Ham* didn't mention anything about this."

I really shouldn't say things like that to my littlest sister. She kicks really hard, and somehow, she seems to never miss my shin at moments like this.

As I hopped on my remaining good leg and held my now aching other leg, the Conductor stepped up beside us.

"Your brother deserved that, perhaps, but it might be best to save it for others who need it more. We will shortly be to what in your day is called Oak Island. When you disembark, you will be facing much worse than a sarcastic older brother. In fact, you will all be facing a danger unlike any you have currently confronted.

"These are pirate waters, and this is the golden era of piracy. And while modern movies such a *Pirates of the Caribbean* glamorize and glorify pirates, I assure you that these men, and a few women, were the most vile and dangerous people on earth. They stole, maimed, tortured, murdered, and lied; nothing was beneath them."

We took it all in, and my mind was racing.

"What is our mission? What child are we here to rescue?"

"Now it is you who are making an assumption, Kyle. That is a dangerous thing. As you go from mission to mission, you will find your duties perhaps expanding from time to time. It is not a child or even a single person you are here to rescue; it is an entire town full of decent people that need your help. Right on the banks of the Molasses Creek is a little settlement, and as it is so near to the Cape Fear River, it is being ravaged by pirates. To be totally accurate, though, I should make that last word singular. It is one pirate in particular that has taken this little settlement as his particular object of terror. In your day that town will have faded into obscurity, and no one will even know that it ever existed. But the residents of Crosstown are dear to the Lord, and He has heard their prayers. And that, Night Heroes, is why you are here."

"I'm not sure I understand," Aly said as she wrinkled up her nose and forehead. "How are we supposed to rescue an entire town and get them away from Pirates? Where will we take them?"

"That is another assumption. You will most assuredly not be able to rescue and remove an entire town..."

The Conductor's voice trailed off as he said that, and I got a very uneasy feeling as I began to sort things out in my mind.

"Working by process of elimination, then, if we are here to save that settlement of people, and they cannot all be moved, the only alternative left to us seems to be to deal with the pirate and his crew. Is that really why we are here?"

The Conductor put his hands on my shoulders and looked into my eyes with an amazing kindness on his face.

"How you do the job is up to you but, yes, it certainly seems like that is the only option left to you."

We let the enormity of that sink in for a moment, then Carrie spoke up.

"You just said, and I quote, 'These men, and a few women, were the most vile and dangerous people on earth. They stole, maimed, tortured, murdered, and lied; nothing was beneath them.' That is a pretty hefty task to deal with."

"Are you scared?" the Conductor asked.

"Of course, we are," I said with no hesitation. We Warner kids have been taught to always be honest, and even if our mom and dad were nearly three centuries away, we would not change in their absence. "But we will do the job anyway."

"Good. And I am glad to see that you have the good sense to be afraid and the honesty to tell the truth about it. A little bit of healthy fear will keep you watchful, and honesty will bring God's blessings."

"Pardon me, sir, but which pirate are we dealing with? The more we know, the more research we can do, and the better we can handle the situation."

The Conductor looked over at Carrie, and for a moment it seemed as if a brief look of fear crossed his face. He turned his back to us and then hung his head. Now that worried me!

"I wish I knew," he whispered.

Chapter Three

I do not think I have ever had a more gut wrenching feeling in my life, not even when we had to free fall out of the plane over Germany. I looked over at Carrie and Aly, and both of them were ashen white. This was most assuredly a new thing, and none of us liked it, not even a little bit. Finally, after what seemed like an eternity, the Conductor raised his head up toward heaven, breathed a heavy sigh, lowered it yet again, and then slowly brought it back up to meet our gaze. He seemed to have aged. He seemed, I guess the best way I could describe it is, weary.

"Children, your parents have raised you to know your Bible. As such, you know that there are no such things as ghosts. But you also know that there are very real spiritual powers all around us, which, no doubt, people who do not understand would surely believe to be ghosts. There are also people who are so evil, so, as your father would say, 'filled with the devil,' that they seem to possess powers and mystery beyond that of just ordinary, sinful people.

"Many pirates in these waters are known entities. I can see them, I know them, I can identify them. These very same pirates are, by and large, seen and known and able to be identified by the people they terrorize. But there is one that is different...

"They call it the Ghost Ship."

We were in broad daylight, but for some reason, all of us jumped and even gasped a little bit when he said that.

"About two years ago, the man and his ship appeared just off the coast of North Carolina. The ship seems so very old, but I assure you it is very powerful. The sails are black, as black as the devil's heart. The vessel seems to make no noise as it cuts through the water, and it always seems to appear out of the fog; no one ever knows that it is coming.

"The cannons never seem to miss, and they tear ships and towns apart like a pack of wolves devouring their prey.

"Crosstown has gotten the worst of it. There are far bigger and wealthier prizes to be taken elsewhere, but, for whatever reason, these few fine folks are the ones he has chosen to terrorize with great regularity."

We were all frightened, but at some point in being scared, fear tends to turn to anger. I could tell by the look on Carrie's face that she was getting there fast.

"Begging your pardon, sir, but where are the authorities in all of this? Why hasn't the government sent ships and men and hunted him down?"

"That is a fair question, young lady, but it is one I suspect you will not like the answer to, even though it will surely tell you why you are here. The governor of North Carolina is, to put it mildly, 'pirate friendly.'"

"You mean he is on the take," Aly said dryly.

"Yes. He is paid handsomely to look the other way while this pirate and many others are pillaging and plundering. These folks can count on no help at all from the government, at least not the government of North Carolina.

"I cannot imagine why God has chosen you for this task, but I trust Him, and I know that you do as well. If He has sent you, then you have within you the capacity to deal with this problem."

"Thank you for those kind words, sir," Carrie said politely. "Any ability we do have is given to us by God, and He can use it and us as He sees fit. If He wants us to deal with a pirate, we will do so. In a way, we already have a leg up on this one, since I already know the pirate alphabet."

That one caught me off guard, and I could tell that it also surprised Aly and the Conductor. But Carrie seemed very serious on this one; her face was totally sober. Until, that is, she began to quote that "alphabet:"

"Ayyyy, Ohhhhh, Arrrr!"

One of the sailors bustling about the desk nearby spit out the mouthful of water he had been attempting to swallow and nearly choked with laughter. The Conductor shook his head back and forth in disbelief.

"You are your father's daughter..." he said with a grin.

"Why, thank you!" she returned brightly.

From there we all fell silent and watched as the shoreline grew ever bigger in our sight. Pirates? Well, why not? After all, we have been taught since childhood that we are not to focus on the size of our problems but on the size of our God. The children of Israel made the mistake of focusing on the size of their enemies when Moses sent twelve spies into Canaan. When they got back, ten of them were focused on the huge people they would have to fight; two of them were focused on the huge God they served.

The people listened to the ten instead of the two, and as a result, they all had to wander around in the wilderness for forty years. I had no desire to end up like that; wasting the bulk of my life because of a "focus problem."

Pirates? Yeah, bring it on...

Chapter Four

As soon as our feet touched the shore, our knees hit the sand. We always made it a point to pray at the start of each day of each mission and at the start of each day in our own time, mission or not. You just simply should not start a day without touching base with heaven. By "doing all you can do," you have simply "done all YOU can do." By praying, you get the power of the God of heaven working on your behalf. Whether it is pirates you are facing, or just a hard subject in school, it is hard to beat that!

Once we finished praying, we stood back up and "pow wowed" for a few minutes. Ever since our adventure in Tennessee, we have been using a lot of old Indian terms. I suspected that by the time this was over we would be speaking in "piratese."

"What's our opening play, Big Bro?" Aly asked with a devious grin.

"Well, I don't think we have to be quite as quiet and careful as last time. It is not likely that the pirates are hiding on the beach or in the woods, and the people in the town are not our enemies. Let's just mosey on out that way, make our way into town, poke around, and see what we can learn."

All things considered, this was a pretty nice way to start a mission. Like my dad, all of us love, love, love the coast. The waves lapping up onto the shore, the birds diving into the water, the breeze blowing through the trees, the salt in the air, what's not to love? We walked a good way down the beach, and then turned slightly left and headed up into the trees. The walking at that point got a bit more difficult; the plant life was as thick as the amazon jungle, having been very much unspoiled by humans.

Nonetheless, after several hours, we got through all of that easily enough. Walking through most anything is fairly simple when neither soldiers nor Indians are trying to kill you. And very soon we were looking out from the trees at what could only very loosely be described by modern standards as a town.

Inn/grub hall. Half completed wooden barricade fence around the edge of the town. Dozens of very crude log houses. Doctor's office. General store. Stable. A dozen or so other nondescript structures. And in the middle of it all, the only building that looked like it could withstand so much as a stiff breeze, a log church.

The town itself showed one construction project that had clearly been started with the best of intentions yet left unfinished. It was an upright log fence such as we often see in some of the old forts we go to visit. What was standing of it had the typical seven or eight-foot-high logs with sharpened points at the top. But the project had clearly been abandoned, and it really wasn't too hard to figure out why.

"That fence wouldn't be much of a help against pirates with cannons and flintlocks. Indians and arrows, yes; that kind of stuff, no."

"Can't argue with you on that, Kyle," Carrie said.

Without another word, we stepped out of the trees and walked into the town. Without even discussing it, we all made our way toward the church.

Up three steps, onto the wooden porch, we took a few breaths, and then walked inside behaving as if we belonged.

There was a cloud of dust in the air. That and a faint swishing sound that stopped within just a couple of seconds of our coming in.

"Welcome, lad and lasses. What brings you into the house of the Lord in the middle of my sweeping and cleaning day?"

The voice was jolly, the face it came from seemed jollier still as the dust settled enough for us to see. This was clearly the pastor, all five foot-two inches of him. He was as bald as a bowling ball and just about as round as one. He had on small round spectacle glasses and some type of an apron.

"Forgive us for bothering you, sir," I said cheerfully and politely. "We came sailing through these parts and heard about your little town, so we thought we would stop in for a while and visit. With a name like Crosstown, it surely sounds like a place that would be hospitable to Christians. We hope so, anyway, since we ourselves are unashamedly followers of the Lord Jesus Christ."

The pastor broke into a grin from ear to ear.

"Well, my, my, my! What a joy it is to hear three young people speak so openly and freely about Christ! I am not certain what level of society you are accustomed to, but as far as I am concerned, I think I can speak for the residents of Crosstown when I say that you are welcome here as long as you sojourn with us. What hospitality we have to offer is at your disposal. Come, let us get you to the inn, and we will arrange a place for you to stay while you are here."

My first reaction was to find a way to kindly refuse his offer, so that we could get off into the trees for our nightly "sleep ride" home. I could tell by the look on Carrie's face that she was thinking the same thing I was. But as I opened my mouth, I heard Aly's voice from beside me.

"That would be simply splendid, Pastor, and we are most grateful. Lead the way, and we shall follow."

You could have knocked me over with a feather.

As the pastor led the way out of the church, we dutifully fell in behind him, me on the right, Carrie on the left, Aly in the middle. Have you ever tried to glare at someone, only to have them look straight ahead and smile as they clearly ignore you? That is what was happening as Carrie and I bored laser beams through our kid sister with our angry eyes. She just looked straight ahead and grinned like a kid unwrapping presents on Christmas morning.

In under a minute we were clop-clopping up another set of old wooden steps, four of them, and entering through the heavy double doors of the inn.

The setting looked much like an old saloon from a cheesy western movie, but I did not see or smell alcohol anywhere. That, I knew, was surely odd by the standards of the time, and it spoke volumes about the influence of a godly little pastor.

There were maybe two dozen people milling about in the room, some eating, some playing odd looking games at the tables, some sitting and talking. In the corner there was a thin-as-a-rail man playing a piano, some oddly Irish sounding tune. He looked much more like an undertaker than a piano man, but I had to admit that he was pretty good. Not as good as mom, but good nonetheless.

The pastor led the way to the counter, and behind it a stout little woman was cleaning pots and pans.

"Sister Mildred," the pastor said, "could you put that down for just a moment, please?"

The little woman laid the current object of her cleaning efforts aside and turned to face the pastor. When she did, her eyes lit upon us, and immediately the "I am everyone's grandmother and you are children so eat, eat, eat" look came over her face. I know that look. Apparently, it has not changed for hundreds, maybe thousands of years. I see it at every church dinner my family and I ever attend. If these sweet little ladies had their way, we would not be able to be the Night Heroes, we would be the Waddling Warriors.

"Oh, hello, Pastor, good day to you. And what beautiful young people have you brought in with you today?"

When she said all of that, I just wish you could have been there. You'll have to trust me on this, and you can ask Carrie and Aly, they will back me up. It was very clear right off the bat that "Sister Mildred" was single, most likely a widow, and that the good pastor was single as well. Sister Mildred was pretty clearly hoping to be Sister Pastor's wife, and the fact that the pastor had "beautiful young people" with him on this particular day had elevated him even further in her estimation. The way she said, "Oh, hello, Pastor, good day to you," was dripping with more honey than a beehive in Winnie the Pooh's Hundred Acre Woods.

The pastor turned beet red. Apparently, he was aware of the good sister's affection and was appropriate enough to be embarrassed by it, though he clearly did not mind.

"These are, well, how incredibly rude of me. I have not even inquired as to your names!"

"That is no problem, Pastor. We are the Warner children. I am Kyle, this is Carrie, and this is Aly," I said, pointing to each sister as I called her name.

"Oh, what lovely names for lovely children!" Sister Mildred cooed. "Pastor, what do you need from me for you or for them on this fine day?"

"Well, Sister, these young people are sojourning here for, dear me! I forgot to ask that as well! How long will you be here, young Mr. Warner?"

"Five days at the longest, Pastor. Our ship will most definitely be here to take us to our next destination by the end of the week."

Looking back, it was very easy for me to determine when the cloud settled in over Sister Mildred's formerly cheerful countenance. When I mentioned our ship coming for us, a darkness, a fear, I believe, came over her face.

"A ship? These are dangerous waters, children, dangerous waters indeed. I do not know what ship is coming for you, but I would not get my hopes up. Not many ships seem to make it through safely anymore, not since..."

Her voice trailed off. She clearly wanted to say it but could not bring herself to do so.

"Sister," the pastor said kindly, "these children need a room for the days they are here. You will simply have to trust the Lord for them beyond that."

"Why, yes, of course, Pastor, of course. They shall have my best room, upstairs and to the right. It overlooks the creek; the view is lovely. At mealtimes, come here to the dining hall and eat with us. There is a back entrance to it, with stairs that will get you to the ground out back, so you can come and go as you need."

"Give me the bill for it all, Sister Mildred," the pastor said. "These children are under my care while they are here."

"Tutt, tutt," Sister Mildred scolded, "I shall do no such thing. They are under your care, but they are under my roof. There will be no bill. Children, you may refer to me as Grandma if you like, and you may think of me as if I am. Now go sit down at a table, and I will bring you your supper."

By our standards it was early for supper, it could not have been more than five o'clock. But darkness came early, and by the time we were done (and about half miserable from devouring the mountain of food "grandma" brought us), we were actually ready for some shut eye!

Pushing back from the table, we thanked Sister Mildred for the supper and went upstairs to our room. It was then that we confronted Aly about her little "indiscretion."

"What were you thinking, Sis? We always go off into the trees somewhere to sleep. Why did you not let me make an excuse to avoid ending up in a room?"

"Well, let me ask you a question, Kyle. Is there any reason that we should go sleep on the ground out in the trees rather than on a bed in a room other than 'because we have always done it that way?'"

And then it hit me: the little squirt was right!

Fifteen minutes later, we were all sound asleep.

Chapter Five

Room 111 of the Econo Lodge. Shallotte. Our day. The sun was streaming in through a tiny gap in the middle of the room darkening shades. The air inside the room was so cold I was sure it must be snowing. Dad had clearly commandeered the AC last night, setting it, as he usually does, at approximately twelve degrees below zero.

"Now wasn't that nice?" Aly chirped quietly yet cheerfully.

"I have to hand it to you, Squirt, that was nice indeed. If we get to go through an entire mission falling asleep in a comfortable bed, we may just end up getting soft and spoiled."

"Maybe, maybe not," Carrie whispered as she quietly joined the conversation. "From the look of 'grandma,' this pirate is really bad news."

"Yeah, and what about how the Conductor looked when talking about him?"

"You both have a point," I said. "We are going to need to be careful."

Within a matter of just a few minutes, mom and dad were up and bustling about, although "bustling" might not be quite a strong enough word for it. With dad, the day starts more as a frenetic, chaotic, pedal to the metal kind of thing.

It did not take us long to scarf down breakfast from the hotel lobby and be out the door for the day. We went to the post office to mail a few things, then checked out a couple of thrift stores. That is absolutely a "parent thing." From there we found an oil change place, got the oil changed and also the tires rotated. Then to a Dollar Tree, then to Walmart where we got some groceries so we could avoid eating out every meal. Back to the hotel, ate lunch there.

We didn't stay long. When there is sand, sea, and sun, we know that dad is going to have us on the beach every single day. Trust me, we kids don't mind! We went to Ocean Isle beach, spent a couple of hours out there just relaxing, splashing in the water, digging in the sand. Man, oh man, that was nice and much needed.

Then a nice kid, a boy maybe twelvish, gave us a perfect Horseshoe Crab!

I was not sure what we were going to do with it, but once we got back to the hotel, we put it out by the pool to dry out so it could stink outside instead of inside. That brought us up to about 4:30, so we went inside to get ready for service.

We got to church an hour or so early and practiced some songs. During this meeting we would all be singing together each night as a family. Mom plays the piano, I play the bass guitar, Carrie sings alto, Aly sings lead, and dad sings bass.

The service went really great. We enjoyed singing, but I really enjoyed the preaching time best. Dad preached on Romans 8:28, a message he calls "When God Mixes Ingredients." Lots of people seemed to get help.

After church we all went down to the Dominos and got great oven roasted sandwiches. We fellowshipped, laughed, cut up, and only knew that we needed to go when they started turning the lights out on us!

A few minutes later we were back at the hotel. And as we went to bed, I was about 99% grateful for the day. That one percent? We had not been given as much as a single moment to do any pirate research.

Chapter Six

"LOOK LIVELY, LADS AND LASSES, SHE'S COMIN AROUND STARBOARD! LOAD THE CANNONS AND FIRE AT WILL!"

We all jumped up gasping; once again the Conductor had given us a less than peaceful morning wake up call.

"You enjoy that, don't you?" Aly asked dryly while Carrie and I shook our heads and started to laugh.

"Well, of course I do, young lady. It is far more enjoyable than having a tooth pulled, taking a final exam, or giving a public presentation, after all."

"I'll take your word on all that," she said from under lowered eyebrows.

"Good morning, Mr. Conductor. Or, should we call you 'Captain' during this mission?"

"Conductor will do just fine, Kyle, but thank you for asking. Are the Night Heroes ready for the second day of this mission?"

"Ready as the sun be to rise in the mornin'," Carrie chimed in with her cheerful pirate voice.

"Good, glad to hear it. You may mull about the deck and lay out your plans for the day, if you like; we are currently forty-five minutes from the coast."

And with that the Conductor headed for the wheel house, leaving us to enjoy and plot and scheme.

The morning aboard ship was lovely, nothing less than a Divine work of art. The sun was peeking over the horizon behind us, and the ship was half-cutting, half-bobbing through the waves, causing a light but pleasant sea spray to dampen our skin. Sea gulls were following alongside, and from time to time a crew member tossed some bit of something edible up into the air for them, causing them to all dive-bomb it at once to see who could snatch it first. The breeze was blowing up from the south, bringing pleasant air from the Gulf of Mexico around the tip of Florida and rushing up the Atlantic coast.

As we leaned out over the edge of the front of the ship, we could see dark figures in the water rushing alongside and just ahead of us. I could not tell if they were dolphins or sharks or something else altogether, but whatever they were, they were fast and graceful.

"What's our play for the day, Matey?" Aly chirped.

"The first thing we do is head back into town. We have our feet in the door, and with both the pastor and "grandma" rallying around us, we should be well regarded enough to ask some innocent sounding questions and see what we can find out."

A bit later we were ashore once again, in roughly the same spot as yesterday. We prayed, then wasted no time in heading back into town. We made it back right around noon and had already decided on heading straight for the church first to see the pastor again.

But the sound of anguished wails from the inn changed our plans, fast.

None of us had to discuss it; we all just ran. Funny, several months ago we likely would have given in to our instincts to run from trouble, but now we automatically ran toward it.

When we burst through the doors, we found Grandma at the table in the center of the room. The pastor was seated beside her, gently patting the back of her hand, a look of anguish on his face. The room was crowded: there were children, women, and a mixture of frightened looking men, and angry looking men.

"Why? Why would our good Lord allow them to take my sweet Lydia? Oh, why!"

"Now, now, Mildred," the pastor cooed, "let us not be too quick to assume that it was the pirates. We have had Indian trouble as well, not to mention that even some of the outlying settlers could be responsible."

"With all due respect, Reverend," a big man with a twirly handlebar mustache interjected, "We've had far more pirate trouble than all other kinds put together." The voice was a thick Irish brogue, and the tone was strained with anger and frustration.

As is so often the case when people are hurting or angry, many voices began to speak at once, and as they did they got louder and louder. They meant well, they really did, but all they were accomplishing was to muddy the waters and delay pursuit.

At the risk of seeming rude, I pushed through the crowd and got down on one knee beside Grandma while the crowd continued to shout at each other. Yesterday we sort of laughed at calling this sweet lady grandma, but as of right now, she was our grandma as far as

I was concerned, and we were going to set things right for her.

"Grandma, you don't know us well yet, but I want you to trust us. Please, as quickly and simply as you can, tell me who is Lydia and what happened to her and when."

"She is the daughter I never had. She came here from Scotland three years ago looking for a new life, and I took her under my wing. She is my world. She is eighteen years old, as pretty as a sunrise, and as innocent as a dove. She comes down early each morning to help me in the kitchen, but she did not come down this morning. Fearing she may be sick, I went up to check on her, but she was gone. Her window was open, but she cannot have jumped. It had to be the pirates; it just had to be. They have taken her to sea, and I will never see my dear Lydia again. Oh, why, God, why?"

And then she broke down in sobbing yet again. For their part, everyone in the room continued to hash and debate what should be done. Some wanted to set out with men and weapons for the shoreline immediately. Others wanted to send inland for help. Some wanted to go and raid the Indians, just in case, and still a few others knew, just knew that it must be some of the settlers from other areas.

I grabbed Carrie and Aly by the hands and dragged them back through the crowd.

Time was wasting, and we needed to get started before those well-intentioned men did. I learned from our last adventure that once people go tromping around, it can be very hard to read sign as you track people.

Once we cleared the doors I let my sisters go and bolted for the back of the inn, with Carrie and Aly right on my heels. When we rounded the back corner, I slid to a stop and held out both of my arms to stop them. Then I very carefully surveyed the setting.

Ten feet past the door that we could use to come out of our room and down the back steps, there was a window, open. That would clearly be Lydia's room. Carefully I took one step at a time toward the ground right underneath it, making sure I did not step on any sign or evidence.

And there was plenty of it.

Six feet from the building, right under the window, were two round indentations in the ground, probably four inches deep, angled upward toward the window.

"Well, that's not too hard to figure out, now is it?" Carrie said with just the smallest hint of anger.

"Nope. Ladder, definitely. And from how deep it got rammed into the ground, it was either a three-hundred-pound man, which is not likely in this era, or a two-hundred-pound man coming down it with a hundred-pound girl over his shoulder.

"Furthermore, we can absolutely, unequivocally, indisputably rule out Indians. Look at all of the tracks. There was no hint of any attempt to mask their coming and going. Can you even imagine Black Crow or any of his warriors being so careless and haphazard?"

"Not a chance," Carrie and Aly said at the exact same time.

"Lastly, we can rule out any 'land lubbers,' settlers or otherwise. Look at the bottom of the two ladder holes."

The girls looked into them, and Carrie beamed, clearly impressed.

"Not bad, Bro, I don't know if I would have caught that. There are grains of salt in each hole. That ladder has spent a lot of time riding around on a ship. So what's the plan?"

"We need to move fast. Those good men in there will eventually decide to act, and we need to be well ahead of them by the time they do. They surely would not realize it, but God has trained and equipped us for this much better than He has them. Let's move, single file. Keep your eyes open as you go, but we can surely afford to move faster than we did when dealing with arrow happy Indians. These pirates are not likely at all to be lying in wait or setting up traps. They will want to get their prey to the ship as soon as possible and be safely out into the waves."

Without another word, we started out in pursuit. It was clear that the trail would not be hard to follow, at least not for us. Those good men back in the inn might struggle with it, but I had no problem following the deep cloppity clop marks of square-heeled pirate shoes, and the path through all of the bent and broken foliage. There had to have been ten men, at least, and they were leaving a trail like a herd of buffalo.

We moved fast, yet quietly. We swatted gnats, we brushed past sticker bushes, we breathed quietly and evenly, but we were keeping up a pace that I wished Falling Rain could see, I think he would have been proud of us. In under an hour we broke out of the trees and onto the beach.

And there was nothing, nothing other than the tracks that led down to the water, and the wide skid-mark that clearly came from a small landing boat that had brought the pirates to shore, then back out to their ship along with Lydia.

"Quick, Aly, give me your binoculars!"

Aly dropped her pack off of her back, whirled around, rammed a hand down into it, and yanked out a small yet powerful set of binoculars. I grabbed them, put them to my eyes, and began to scan the waters. With the good time we had made, surely we could still spot the ship somewhere out on the waves.

But there was nothing, absolutely nothing.

"Kyle?"

"Not now, Carrie, I need to find that ship; I need to see which way it is going."

"I think you would be better served to see this instead."

She sounded urgent, and as calm as she normally is, that got my attention. I pulled the binoculars away from my eyes and looked over at her. She was pointing, so I followed down her arm, which was pointing at a tree about fifteen feet away. While I had been intent on the horizon, my brilliant sister had scanned our surroundings.

There was a note on the tree, driven in with a couple of rusty nails.

Laydees and gents o Crosstown,
Greetings from the Ghost Ship.
Thank ye kindly for the new
galley maid, we do get so tired
o swabbin our own deks.
Rest assured, we will
be treatin her exactly
as ye might expect us to.
Or, if ye'd like ta have her
back unharmed, have ten strong
men tied up securely on the
beach at sunset tomoro.
We'll be glad to exchange
the maid for ten good dekhands.
We shall come ashore to make
the exchange at last light
tomoro. Don't displease us,
we dasnt like to be displeased.
Kindest regards, the Captain

Chapter Seven

"Those seafaring punks must be getting bored," Carrie snapped angrily, "or they would have just marched into town with guns leveled and taken whomever they want. It looks like they feel the need to spice things up a bit."

"I would say you are correct, Sis. But hopefully that will work to our advantage. We surely cannot muster enough firepower to withstand an all-out assault from them; I doubt if we could do that even if every man in town was willing and able and armed. But with them toying with everyone this way, maybe, just maybe we can turn the tables. The first thing we need to do, though, is get this note back into town. Whether we like it or not, it would not be right to keep it from them, even if it would possibly be easier to do things on our own."

Aly nodded in agreement, and like a flash we were off, hoofing it back to town. When we arrived, we came around front of the inn and made our way in through the double doors once again. The crowd had thinned considerably, there were maybe half a dozen men still there along with the pastor, grandma, and a couple of young boys. Grandma was still at the table, and she and the pastor were both bowed in earnest prayer.

But a few seconds after we came in, we heard them both say a quiet "amen," and then the two of them looked up at us with eyes red from crying as they prayed.

"Children, I am sorry, in my grief I have failed to tend to you today," grandma said as she sniffed and brushed a tear from her cheek. "What can I do for you?"

"Nothing, ma'am, but I surely hope that we can do something for you. While everyone was in here debating what to do, we went out back and did a little investigating. We found evidence that Lydia was taken out of her room by a ladder, and we followed a good many tracks all the way down to the sea shore. When we arrived, we found this."

I handed her the note, and she pulled a small set of glasses out of her apron pocket and put them low on her nose. For a couple of moments she read, her hands trembling ever the more as she did. The pastor read over her shoulder, and I could see a righteous indignation beginning to show on his face.

"Why?" she said as she laid the note down on the table. "They could steal men from any number of ships that they take at sea. Why would they do this? Why have we become the special object of their vile attentions?"

"Grandma," I said slowly, "evil men do not think or behave or conduct themselves as good men do. Abel brought an excellent offering to God from the blood of an animal, Cain killed his brother as if he was an animal. Evil cannot be charted, because it recognizes no legitimate boundaries."

"You are wise beyond your years, young man," the pastor said with a thin smile. "Thank you for what you have done. I must now ring the church bells and assemble the men; we have some decisions to make."

The pastor pushed away from the table and headed out the doors, down the street, and toward the church. A few moments later we heard the church bell begin to peal, and we along with Grandma Mildred got up and headed over there. People were pouring out of buildings and joining us as we went, and I knew that many would be coming from out of the hills and hollows of the surrounding woods as well.

We made our way back up the wooden stairs and into the church and followed

Grandma down to the very front row. The pastor stood silently behind the pulpit. I knew that he would not begin until everyone had arrived.

It took about fifteen minutes. The church was filled to capacity, with many people actually standing around the walls.

"Good people of Crosstown," he began in a very pastoral voice, "most of you by now are surely aware that our town family has once again been attacked in the night. The assault came much more subtly this time, but the wound left is by far the worst we have yet endured. Up until now we have merely had goods and wealth and peace of mind taken from us. Now, one of our very own has been taken, and it may well be that the only way to get her back is by losing even more."

And then he read the note. As he did, I was looking over my shoulder to see everyone's reaction. As with any church and any situation, the reaction was mixed. Some were clearly angry, some terrified, a few seemed to take it in stride as yet another fact of life. As the pastor finished, the reaction began.

"And what do you think we should do, Pastor? Shall we once again send to the governor for help? Or shall we, this time, call him out publically as the wretched friend of thugs and criminals that he is?"

The voice had a thick German accent to it and was laced with an "I told you so" air.

The pastor slowly pulled his glasses off of his face, looked down at the ground for just a second or two, and then raised his eyes, then his head, to face the man. He looked at him eye to eye briefly, then panned his head from one side of the crowd to the other.

"Beloved, Scripture tells us to honor the king..." as he said it, I could hear a murmur begin to rise. The pastor heard it too and raised his volume just a notch or two to compensate, "but it also says in Proverbs 25:19 'Confidence in an unfaithful man in time of trouble is like a broken tooth, and a foot out of joint.'"

When he said that, the assemblage fell utterly quite, and the pastor then continued in his normal tone, "We cannot look to the governor for help. We can look to the Lord for help, and we can do all that we can do ourselves in conjunction with that. Scripture does not describe faith as being a lazy thing. Noah had faith, yet it was his hands and the hands of his sons that physically built the ark. David had faith, yet it was his hand that wielded the sling. Jesus instructed His own disciples to sell their garments to buy a sword. We will pray, yes, we will always pray. But we will, we must, act as well."

"But what are we to do?" came a high pitched, nasally sounding voice from the rear. "They are pirates, they have weapons, cannons, cutlasses. Are we to take up pitchforks and a few muskets against them? They have taken one person, just one. I say let them have her, and maybe that will suffice them."

"It most certainly will not, and how dare you give up a precious girl without a fight! Where I come from, men have more backbone than that!"

My jaw dropped, and I leaped up to stop her. It was Aly; standing on her tiptoes to be seen, and with an angrier look on her face than I had ever observed in all her eleven years. She brushed me away, refusing to be stopped.

"Well? Anybody?"

It was the pastor who got her quieted.

"Young lady, thank you for your passion. You serve as a good reminder to us all. When the adults failed to act, it was a lad named David who rescued them all. But hopefully that will not be necessary here. Congregation, it is up to us to act, one way or the other. Our young guest is correct. We cannot simply give Lydia up without trying to get her back.

"As I see it, we have two options. One, we can try to find and attack them. This option seems, to me at least, to have little chance of success. Or two, we can do as they ask and have ten men volunteer to give themselves for her. I myself will be the first volunteer. Are there nine others?"

Four men stood to their feet. Four good, godly, Christ-like men.

"Five will not be enough," the pastor said. "Are there any others?"

The room fell silent. Deathly, utterly, frighteningly silent.

Chapter Eight

After probably twenty seconds of silence, when it was evident that no one was going to stand up or speak up, I did.

"Pastor, may I say a word?"

"Certainly, young man, since it seems that no one else is going to."

"There may be a third option, since it seems that option number one will not work and option number two does not appear palatable to anyone. These pirates have stolen one from among you. You are used to behaving honorably, but these are not honorable men you are dealing with. That being the case, you need to view them as enemies to be defeated, not as brothers to be reasoned with.

"Out on the sea, they have the advantage. But once ashore the playing field is leveled a bit. I suggest that you use the time and the terms they have given you to your advantage. The goal, though, must be bigger than you think. Getting Lydia back, even if you could do so without giving any men in exchange, will not solve your problem. If you cannot cut the head off of the snake, it will continue to strike. You must use this opportunity to deal with the captain himself."

The room immediately erupted. It would be pointless for me to even try to tell you what all was said, since it was mostly just everyone shouting at one time, thus producing an unintelligible cacophony. Basically, though, the general message sent by the shouting was something along the lines of, "You have lost your cotton-picking mind, boy; we are no match for them; go away."

The shouting continued until a very large noise came from a very small man. It was the pastor using his "shout aloud like Isaiah" voice.

"Silence, NOW!"

The room fell quiet.

"Thank you. Brethren, you are forgetting your Scripture. Proverbs 18:13 says, 'He that answereth a matter before he heareth it, it is folly and shame unto him.' I grant you, the young man's plan seems, er, impossible. But if we are to follow Scripture, even in this we must hear what is suggested before we judge either for or against it. Kyle, what exactly are you proposing?"

"Pastor, you must take what you know about evil men and use it against them. What was the very first sin?"

"Eatin' the fruit!" Came a deep and heavily accented voice from the back. But just as quickly, the pastor corrected him.

"No, Paul, you are incorrect. The first sin was the sin of Lucifer, pride. And that sin has been at the core of every sin man has committed since."

"Exactly, Pastor. And when dealing with pirates, you are dealing with, no pun intended, a boat-load of pride. Anything that makes a captain look bad in front of his men is a sign of weakness that is liable to cause a mutiny. The captain of this 'Ghost Ship' doubtless wants to get his men without getting his hands dirty. We cannot give him that luxury.

"As much as you want to get Lydia back immediately, you must wait at least one more day. The pirates left you a note? Well, leave them one of your own, a counter proposal. Make it absolutely huge, something that is able to be seen by spyglass from well out to sea, because they will definitely check things out before they come ashore.

"Tell them that you think the captain is a coward being allowed to lead brave men, otherwise he would come ashore himself. Tell him you will give him his ten men, as long as he comes ashore personally with ten, and only ten of his own men to get them.

"Get ten men ready to pretend to be exchanging themselves. But have the beach set up as a trap to capture the captain and the men who come ashore and regain your Lydia.

"You will have the advantage of surprise, I think. Have you ever fought back before?"

The silence in the room and the people looking furtively one at another gave me my answer.

I knew that this was not an easy choice. I was basically asking pacifists to fight and to do so against blood-thirsty killers. I also knew that, even though I would like to stay and put pressure on them, the Holy Spirit was nudging my heart, demanding that I remember His authority, and give Him room to work. He is, after all, the one responsible for convicting the hearts of men, as my dad always says.

"Pastor, good people of Crosstown, my sisters and I will leave you now to give you time to talk and to decide. If you choose to go through with this, we will help you. We will retire to our room for the night and will be back here in the church early tomorrow morning. Please be here to let us know your decision."

And with that, we Night Heroes quietly walked out of the church to let God do His work.

Chapter Nine

We had gone to sleep in our quaint little upper room, and I had awakened to the smell of my littlest sister's foot hanging over the edge of the bed back at room 111 of the Econo Lodge.

I rolled over to remove my nose from the olfactory offending appendage, and silently began my day in prayer. I prayed for the situation so long ago yet so near to us in Crosstown. Funny, now that I think of it; I was praying for something a couple of hundred years in the past. That made me wonder, would prayer in our time affect the outcome of what would happen in the past?

But why wouldn't it? After all, God operates outside of time. But if that was the case, would it have any impact if I prayed for my loved ones who had already died that I feared may have been lost? That thought made my head spin: could it be that my prayers in my time would be heard by God, resulting in Him convicting someone in the past, resulting in them, unbeknownst to me, accepting Christ on their deathbed?

And so I prayed some more, this time for my loved ones who had gone on that I was not sure of. Then I prayed for mom and dad, and our home church and our great pastor, and I prayed for the revival meeting.

Soon enough dad was up, and therefore we were up too. We rushed and got up, got dressed, ate breakfast in the lobby, then headed out for a day of adventure. As I suspected (and hoped), today was a history day for dad. And, most gratefully, dad wanted to go down the road to the great little town of Southport to the Maritime Museum. I knew that would give us the opportunity to do some much-needed pirate research.

It took us about forty-five minutes, once we got into the Yukon, to get to Southport. If you ever go there on a Sunday or Wednesday, be sure to drop in at the Sonrise Baptist Church, which is pastored by Brother Rodney Cox. Great man, great church, we have been there many times.

Dad pulled the Yukon into the parking lot, and we all headed on inside. Boy, oh boy, talk about a cool place, and also a (once again, no pun intended) treasure trove of information. Well, here, see for yourself:

Photo by Rodney & Christina Cox

Photo by Rodney & Christina Cox

Photo by Rodney & Christina Cox

Photo by Rodney & Christina Cox

Photo by Rodney & Christina Cox

On the way out I went through the bookstore and bought two great books with a lot of information and history about pirates. I knew those were likely to come in very handy.

It was about lunch time, and, as happens so often, my dad's nose led us to our destination. It was right on the main road leading out of Southport, and as the smell of barbecue jumped in through our rolled down windows, I knew the vehicle would be making a left into the parking lot of Big Al's Slam Dunk Barbecue.

The food was really, really (did I mention really?) good. And Big Al, the owner, is really, really big, as in about six foot seven! And the slam dunk part? Well, he played Basketball at the University of Tennessee! That is way cool, since UT is my favorite team. That does, though, put me at odds with the rest of the family, who are Alabama all the way in football, and UNC all the way in basketball. Philistines.

Once we were done there we headed back to Shallotte. Carrie used the time in the vehicle to speed read the pirate books, stopping to slow-read the parts that may be helpful to us. Once we got to the hotel, we grabbed our stuff and headed out to Sunset Beach just a few miles away. We only had an hour or so, then we had to get back to the hotel and get ready for church.

I got ready pretty quick, then while everyone else was getting ready I scanned the books.

Once we were all washed and gussied and dressed better than a Thanksgiving turkey, we headed on over to Victory. The service was great, as I had hoped and prayed for. Dad preached a salvation message called "Seven Days Too Late." One young lady got saved, which is, bar none, the most important thing anyone can ever do.

After church a bunch of us went down to the Dairy Queen and got brain freeze and a serious case of the giggles. The kids, at least. The adults smiled a lot, but dad at least is definitely not a giggler.

Soon it was time to retire for the night, so we said our goodbyes and headed back to the Econo Lodge. We prayed, hugged, and bedded down, mom and dad to a good night of rest, and us kids hopefully to a night/day of pirate bashing.

Chapter Ten

We woke to the warm feeling of the sun shining on our faces and the gentle rocking of the waves. That was a bit of a surprise. Based on the last two days, I had expected a loud, pirate-style wake up call.

I sat up and then nudged Carrie and Aly. They sat up themselves, rubbed their eyes, and shook the cobwebs of out their heads. Carrie yawned really big, then we all stood up and looked around the deck.

The sailors were still milling about doing their jobs as they had been on the previous days of the mission, but the Conductor was nowhere to be seen.

"Well, that's odd," Aly said from the side of a wrinkled-up mouth. "What happened to our megaphone morning greeting, and where is the Conductor?"

"I don't know, Squirt, but this surely strikes me as odd. Excuse me," I said to one of the deck hands, "where is the Conductor, um, I mean the captain?"

The deck hand did not say a word, he just jabbed his thumb backwards and nodded his head over toward the wheelhouse and kept on walking,

"Well, what say we head on up there and see what gives?"

"Good choice, Carrie. Let's head that way."

We scurried across the deck, our sea legs were getting pretty good, up a few flights of stairs, and shortly we were in front of the wheelhouse door. I suspected it was not like any other wheelhouse door on the sea; for there, front and center at eyeball level, was a simple cross etched on the door.

"I doubt if the Ghost Ship has one of those," Aly said simply.

"No, not likely. But it surely would help. There is nothing as powerful as a reminder of the cross and what Jesus did on it. Anybody who really focuses on it cannot help but be changed."

We knocked on the door and immediately heard the voice of the Conductor from within beckoning us to enter, so we did.

"Good morning, sir, we were surprised not to see you about on deck this morning."

"Sorry about that, Kyle, but I am incredibly pre-occupied right now. Things don't feel right: the wind, the waves, it is all just...odd. When it gets like that, it always makes me feel better to have my hands on the wheel."

"I understand that, sir. It is kind of like in basketball. If my team is down late, I want the ball, I want to be the one running the show and/or taking the last shot."

"That must be a male thing," Aly said with a shake of her head.

"Perhaps," the Conductor replied, "but it still makes me feel better. And you will just have to trust me; I have been around the sea for a very long time, and something does not feel right. It very much feels like, well, a sea a very long time ago that always seemed to have supernatural storms fall on it at all the wrong times, or right times, depending on your perspective."

We all fell silent as we mused on that. What were we dealing with? A ghost ship, though none of us believed in ghosts. A town being terrified for no particularly good reason, since there were much richer targets elsewhere. A girl being kidnaped, ostensibly in exchange for ten men, when it would have been much easier for the pirates just to take what men they wanted. Our Conductor, whose instincts we had learned to trust, uncomfortable and uncertain. I could not help but reflect on how bad of an ingredient list that made for.

The ship cut through the water with great precision and power, and shortly we were on shore once more. We took time to pray, and then headed back into town.

When we arrived, we did as we had said we would do, and made straight for the church. Sure enough, everyone was gathered. As we walked in, the pastor spoke up immediately.

"Welcome, children. We do appreciate you coming. It seems as if everyone is here."

"I am glad to see that, Pastor. What decision have you made?"

"If you are willing to help, the people of Crosstown are willing to try your approach."

That was good, very good. I smiled just a bit as I thought of a surprised and disappointed pirate captain. Still, we had been through enough to know that things do not always go as planned, so we would have to be careful, very, very careful.

"Then I suggest we get started immediately," I said. "Get two or three men to make the sign I suggested. Pick out ten men to serve as the decoys, and, Pastor, you lead them. Every other man comes with us. Grab every weapon you have, and anything else that can even remotely be used as a weapon: sticks, axes, clubs, hammers, anything. As soon as you have that, meet me in front of the inn.

"Ladies, there are a few things you can do as well. I need rough fabric: muslin, burlap, that type of thing, and as many pins as you have.

"And one last thing. We start with prayer."

Chapter Eleven

After we prayed for God's help and success in our plan, everyone rushed out of the church in a mad beehive kind of activity. Soon the groups were set and ready, the weapons on hand, and the materials in a cart.

The trip back through the trees to the beach took a good while this time. For starters, there were a lot of people involved. Secondly, I was making sure that everyone stayed quiet, and that there was not a lot of rustling of the small trees. I did not want some pirate out to sea with a spyglass wondering why the jungle looked like a pack of elephants was coming through it.

Grandma and all of the other ladies along with all of the town children were in the church praying, under her direction. We would need that more than anything.

After what seemed like an eternity, we made it to the edge of the trees. I held up my hand for everyone to silently stop, and they did.

"Give me just a minute, please," I whispered, "let me check things out with my, um, two eyed spyglass."

I reached into my pack and retrieved my binoculars. Better technology would surely be an advantage for us.

For a long while I scanned the water all the way to the horizon and back, and on either side of a couple of tiny islands a good ways off.

"It is clear. Everyone do as I instructed, immediately and quickly."

God bless the people, they may not have understood all of my methods, but they were eager to try anyway. A few men put the sign up, and I had to admit, it was a doozy. Fully six-feet tall and eight feet wide, it would be guaranteed to catch our pirate's attention. The other men worked in smaller groups. I had them put sticks in the ground and then cover the sticks with the fabric. Then Carrie and Aly showed them how to take branches and leaves from the trees and pin them to the fabric. Within a couple of hours, the camouflage was so good that I suspected even a modern-day hunter would be impressed!

"Hey, Kyle," Carrie grinned, "do you ever wonder if the things we do now affect the future? I wonder if one of these folks' grandchild will be the official inventor of camo, after what we have shown them how to do?"

"That would be cool," Aly chimed in. "Maybe if we can prove it, we can collect the royalties!"

Finally, we were set, with a couple of hours to go until sunset. Our decoys were "tied" to trees, but not really. All of the men in town were hiding behind the camo barriers, waiting. Now we would do what I hated most...wait.

"Pssst, Pastor!"

I nearly jumped out of my skin when the voice spoke from right behind me. I wheeled around, and there was a woman behind me with a frantic look on her face.

"What do you need, Sis?" I asked

"Pastor needs to come at once, Sister Mildred has suddenly fallen ill!"

I groaned to myself. Every man would be needed, but I knew the pastor's first priority at this exact moment would be to tend to this dear sister, since no one would interrupt us unless it was truly serious.

I slid quietly over to the tree to which the pastor was "tied."

"Pastor, we have a problem. A lady from town is here, and she says that Sister Mildred is sick, and you need to come at once. Have another man take your place and go."

I could see at once the horrified and torn look on his face. I remember my dad listening to a preacher preach once who said, "Duties never conflict." Dad, always a logical and honest sort, twisted up his eyes and face in a sort of scrunched up, disapproving way. When I asked him about it later, he said, "Try telling that to a pastor who has two members having open heart surgery on the same day at the same time in hospitals fifty miles apart!"

The pastor of the good folks of Crosstown was at just such a moment, but I knew I could help him with it.

"Pastor, go, and don't worry. I can handle things here. You go tend to Sister Mildred; leave this to me."

It took some convincing, but finally he scurried off back into the trees. I said a silent prayer for him, and for Grandma, and for Lydia, and for us. I prayed for the pirates, too. I prayed that the pirate captain himself would be the one that I got to deal with, and that I would have the privilege of shattering his jaw for him. Spiritual? I'm not really sure, but I do know that God already knows what I am wanting anyway, so I may as well not be dishonest about it.

The waiting is always the worst part of all. Running is no trouble; we are good at it. Fighting is definitely no trouble; we are good at it, and we enjoy it. But waiting? Waiting I don't like, not even a little.

I had to admit, though, that if one has to wait around, this certainly was a nice place to wait. The breeze and the salt air were cool and pleasant, the fragrance of paradise seemed to waft all around us, and the sounds of the sea birds was like a symphony of the highest order. How, I wondered, could such evil even bear to touch a place like this?

We waited.

We waited a while longer.

I could see our decoys were getting antsy.

"What in the world is taking them so long, Kyle? Shouldn't they be here by now?"

"I don't know, Aly, I surely thought they would. But there are just a few more minutes till sundown, and I don't see any movement out there."

I scanned the horizon with my binoculars, and there was nothing, absolutely nothing. Unless the ghost ship was now invisible, it did not look to be coming.

"Yer grand plan dasn't seem ta be a workin," came the thick whispered voice of a gentleman off to my left.

"No, it doesn't, at least not yet."

But it was then that "not yet" clearly became "not at all," for at that moment the sun sank fully beneath the horizon. I stood up and walked out onto the beach, and Carrie and Aly were right beside me.

"What happened, Big Bro?"

"I don't know, Squirt, I don't know. But something tells me we better get back to town."

The sight that followed, an entire town of dejected and confused people following us back through the jungle, was not pleasant. What in the world had gone wrong? Why had they not come?

As it was quickly getting dark, the trip back into Crosstown was slow. Finally, though, the torches lit the edge of the town, and we all made our way to the church. We filed inside, and as I surveyed the ladies and children waiting for us, I got two of the biggest shocks of my life. The first shock was Sister Mildred, sitting up front, clearly as healthy as a horse. The second shock was far worse; the pastor was nowhere to be seen, and everyone was looking at us as if we were still supposed to have him.

The next few minutes were pure pandemonium, with everyone trying to talk at once, argue over top of each other, and worst of all, lay pretty much all of the blame on us! It took us a good while, and a lot of grandmotherly influence from Sister Mildred to get everyone quieted down enough for us to speak and try to figure out exactly what had happened. But when the light finally clicked on over my head, it stunned even me.

"Where is the lady that came looking for the pastor?"

She was nowhere to be found, absolutely nowhere. When I described her, voices started popping up at once. Finally, one voice spoke for all of them, "Susanna, Susanna Mattson. She got to Crosstown just a few weeks before the pirates started terrorizing us."

Now that, friends, is what I would call "a clue."

It did not take us long to piece things together from there, at least as far as we could take them. Clearly, Susanna was somehow in league with these pirates, and as such, had warned them of our plans. But as for the rest, why she had come for the pastor, and where he was, I had a very, very bad feeling about that...

For now, there was little that we could do other than all of us go to our homes or places to get some sleep. The ball was clearly in the pirate's court, and we were left with no real option other than to wait to hear from them. They clearly had something big in mind and were not yet done. They would contact us again, of that we were certain.

Chapter Twelve

We woke once again to the icy confines of our hotel room. Carrie was already up, sitting in a chair with her knees curled up to her chest, resting her head on them.

I slipped over to her and sat down on the floor beside her.

"What's up, Sis?" I whispered. "What's going through your mind?"

"I am angry and upset. Things haven't gotten any better since we arrived, they have gotten worse. And now the pastor has been taken! If we fail him, Kyle, I don't think I can live with that."

"Relax, Sis, we still have two days to work. Besides, you know as well as I do how tough pastors are. They may seem meek and mild, but I never knew a good man of God yet who didn't have a backbone like a saw log.

Taking him may well be the biggest mistake those pirates have ever made."

It didn't take long for our day to be in full swing. We did the traditional tooth brushing and hair fixing and face poofing (the girls, not us guys) and soon were up and out the door. We grabbed a quick bite from the lobby on the way out, but not too much. Today we would be having lunch with a sweet lady named Toni Howard who lives about an hour away.

We went and picked Mrs. Toni up and took her to one of her favorite places, the Boundary House. It was really good. They serve fish, steaks, ribs, about anything you could want. A touch expensive, but worth it for a rare treat. The fellowship was the best part; it always is.

Well, we took Mrs. Toni back home, and then went back to the hotel just long enough to get changed, then back out to the beach. We walked and splashed and played, and while we were at it, I noticed dad and mom talking to some man we did not know.

"One guess what they're doing," Carrie grinned as she swam up beside me.

"One guess is all it would take," I said. "They are talking to him about the Lord, and inviting him to church."

Sure enough we were right. His name was Mr. Prince, and we all spent a few minutes later praying for him.

We stayed out on the beach for a couple of hours, and along the way managed to find some great sand dollars. But all too soon it was time to head back to the hotel and get ready for service. We rinsed off, got rid of as much sand as we could, loaded back up into the Yukon and got back over to the hotel. From there it was a quick barrage of showers, stylings, dressings, and then some quiet time praying and reading our Bibles, getting our hearts ready for service.

We got back over to Victory at about 6:15 and spent a little while practicing a few songs. Service started promptly at 7:00, and it was a good one. Dad preached a message called "The Things the Enemy Cannot Take." It was all about Isaac, and how the Philistines fought him over the wells of water that his father Abraham had dug so many years earlier.

The Philistines had at some point filled them up with dirt. When Isaac went to re-dig them, each time he succeeded, they came and fought with him over the well, claiming it belonged to them.

Isaac, though, just kept moving and digging, and kept on hitting water. You see, what the Philistines, and even Isaac did not know, was that they were digging into something called the Mountain Aquifer. The Philistines were able to take his wells, but a well is nothing more than a hole in the ground! They could not take all of his shovels, they could not take his determination to keep digging, and above all they could not take his water. 3,500 years later, in our modern day, that Mountain Aquifer still produces one third of all the water in the land of Israel!

God's supply is always so much bigger than we know. And, somehow, that thought became a quick comfort to me while dad was preaching it. My sisters and I were facing off against a formidable foe, one who seemed to have all of the advantages. But our God is bigger by far than those pirates.

I went to the altar during the invitation that night. No one, no matter how long they have been saved, should ever feel too big or too "holy" to go to the altar and pray.

While I was there, I quickly felt something on my left and on my right. Aly was on one side, Carrie was on the other. We made quick eye contact and then went right to prayer. None of us had to ask what any of the rest were praying for, since all of us already knew.

After service we went to Dairy Queen again, this time with some good friends of ours, Pastor Bryan Burr and his family. They had come from more than an hour away to be in the meeting with us. That was awesome and reminded us again how precious good friends are.

But soon enough we were done, back at the hotel, bedded down, and ready for another good night of what my parents would call sleep and what we would call adventure.

Chapter Thirteen

The waves were far rougher than before, and a strong sea mist was breaking over the bow of the ship. My eyes opened to gray skies, and the ocean was sounding far more agitated than it had on previous days.

"Good morning, Night Heroes," the Conductor said without even turning toward us. He was at the rail about ten feet from us, looking out at the waves and the sky.

All of us joined him at the rail.

"Good morning, sir. I guess you know that things have not gone very well thus far."

"Yes, Kyle, I know. But as you told your sisters, you still have two days to work. The condition of those days, though," and as he said this he turned a weathered eye toward the gathering clouds, "may be in question. The weather seems to be taking a turn, and I cannot help but feel something ominous to it."

None of us could argue with that, we all felt pretty much the same way.

After a hour or so of rough sailing, we were once more ashore. Though we felt the need for urgency, we dared not spare on our prayer time to begin the day. The great old preacher of yesteryear, Charles Spurgeon, once said, "Prayer is the slender nerve that moveth the muscles of omnipotence."

If we ever needed that omnipotent power of God to go to work for us, it was now, and so we prayed. We prayed fervently, long, and honestly, laying bare our fear before God, and asking for His help and victory to overcome this maddening and elusive foe we faced. We thanked God for Calvary, and for the blood He shed there to cleanse us from our sin. We prayed for the pastor, and for Lydia, and for the good people of Crosstown. We prayed that our adversaries would make mistakes, and that we would be able to capitalize on them.

Once we said amen, we were up and running for the town. In the absence of the pastor people were sort of walking around in a daze, not really knowing what to do, or who to follow.

That last part I had no choice but to fix, and quickly. These folks could not be wandering about like sheep without a shepherd, or they would most certainly get eaten by these sea going wolves.

We made our way through the crowd and over to the church. Without so much as asking, I grabbed the rope of the bell and began to pull it like I was trying to yank it down. The bell pealed loud, long, and clear. After seven or eight tugs, I turned and walked inside with Aly and Carrie right behind me. They instinctively took seats, Aly on the front row to the far left and Carrie on the back row on the far right.

That's good, guys, I thought to myself. *Spread out so as to be able to respond from different angles to any threat. Nice.*

Within eight or ten minutes, everyone in the town had gathered into the church. No one seemed to register any opposition to me standing behind the pulpit. No one there would do it, but everyone needed someone to do so.

"Good people of Crosstown," I began, "last night the enemy struck, utilizing the help of a traitor among you. It should not surprise anyone that the devil would use such a tactic, since even our Lord was betrayed by one of His closest men.

"But the question is, what to do now. I expect that the pirates either have or will be sending you a message as to what they expect."

"Tis already done, lad," came an Irish brogue from the back of the room. "I awoke early this mornin ta find a message down by the creek; a rather pointed message."

Everyone in the room looked over at him unsure what he was talking about.

"Ya better just come see, all of ye."

Without another word he arose and walked out, and everyone, including us Night Heroes, fell in behind him. We could hear whispers as he walked, and the general information in them was that we were heading toward his house, which was right by the Molasses Creek.

It took maybe four minutes of hard walking, but soon we entered what I guess was considered the yard of a small cabin. There was no grass, no fence, but merely an area worn down from walking. The man did not stop out front or go into his house. He strode around back, and as all of us followed, a gasp worked through the crowd like the wave at a big ball game.

There, right by the banks of the creek, was a cross.

On that cross, someone had nailed a message, and it didn't surprise anyone to find out who.

Ladies and gents O Crosstown, greetins to ye all. By now ye surely know that we have yer dear pastor, along with our new galley maid. Twas so kind of ye to inform our spy of yer plans. But seein as how that didn't work out so well for ye, maybe ye'll not be tryin anythin else so foolish. I'm sure ye all wonder jest why we've chosen ye as the special objects of our attention.

Never let it be said that we pirates are simply men interested in women and wealth. On the contrary, some of us are a rather philosophical lot, especiallymeself. Tis yer name that craws me, that and the fact that it fits. All of ye be nothin more than worthless followers of the cross, and the one I serve takes great umbrage ta that. Tis he from whom I get me power, and tis he what has directed me to terrorize yer pathetic little town. Does there seem ta be no rhyme or reason to our madness? Good, that is the way I want it. Tis my desire for ye ta fear every day, to feel loss and pain that cannot be explained, and ta finally blaspheme yer pathetic God.

I know that ye have some newcomers among ye, a young man and two young lasses, who are tryin ta lead ye agin us. You tell them that I will be dealin with them shortly.

In closin, I'm sure ye want to know what our terms are, and what we expect from ye. In short, the answer is, absolutely nothin. There is nothin ye can do, or say, or give to keep us from ye. I get no greater joy outta life than makin yer lives miserable, and I will continue ta do so in the most erratic and unreasonable ways possible. I am the wicked cat, and ye all are nothin more than mice fer me ta play with.

Regards,
Captain Edward Low

A murmur began to go through the crowd. The murmur quickly grew to a crescendo of hopelessness, with people actually wailing in surrender and terror. But that crescendo was brought to a screeching halt by a loud voice, one that I knew oh, so well, that of my sister Carrie.

"STOP THAT!"

The effect was amazing and instantaneous.

"Do you not see what is happening, any of you? How long has your pastor preached to you? How many times have you heard sermons on spiritual warfare? Do you not remember that the devil is your adversary, a roaring lion seeking whom he may devour?

"Do you not remember the command of Ephesians chapter six that we put on the whole armor of God and stand against him? Do you not remember the heroes of the faith in Hebrews eleven? Have you forgotten a little shepherd boy that faced off against a giant and won? Our God has not changed! This pirate is no better than Goliath, and we are no worse than David.

"Fight! Fight back! If these devils want to march against the armies of the cross, then give them an army to march against, not a bunch of cowering victims."

"But what are we to do?" came a hopeless female voice from near the front.

"The first thing we have to do is find them," I said. "They clearly used the Molasses Creek here as an entry point for a small boat to put up this cross and send this message, and I would be willing to bet that is also how they spirited away the pastor last night."

"That ship cannot be far from shore. My sisters and I will go straight up the creek to the ocean. Half of you take the northern side and do the same, the other half take the southern side. Be quick, as it is not likely they are too far ahead of us."

"How do you know?" asked an old man near the back.

"Because," I said "the mud has not yet settled totally in the eddy where they came ashore and then put back out. They may be a few hours ahead of us at best, so hurry!"

God bless them, they all immediately did as I asked. They did not really have much of a clue what to do other than that, but what they were doing would be enough. I did not expect them to be the ones to deal with this pirate, clearly, that is what we were here for. I just needed help pinning down his location.

Carrie and Aly were already ahead of me, running down the creek bank, and sometimes out into the creek itself. For a while I could hear noise in the woods on either side of me as the town folks worked their way through the trees, but soon we had far outdistanced them.

It did not take us long to get to shore, and this time, urged on by the need for speed, we simply burst out into the open. I quickly rammed my hand into my pack and grabbed my binoculars and did a quick scan of the water.

Nothing.

"Kyle, look!"

It was Aly, and she was pointing away from the water. I hurriedly turned to see what she was pointing at, and gasped when I did. Most of the area as a flat as a pancake, but there was one nice tall outcropping maybe a mile from us, a perfect place for a better view.

Without a word we all ran. My best official time ever in the mile is right at five minutes, and I am pretty sure I did even better than that. Carrie and Aly were maybe half a minute behind me as I rushed up the slope. I got to the top, yanked up the binoculars once again...

And bingo.

"She is heading northwest, heading straight across the Southport channel for Battery Island!"

"That makes sense," Carrie said through gasps of breath, "It would be a perfect spot to hide. Easy access both to the open sea and to the Cape Fear River, yet sheltered from storms."

I watched until the ship disappeared from view against the land of the island.

"This is better news than I would have hoped for, guys. That island is no more than a couple of miles away. Those pirates are clearly counting on us not being able to get there, but I guarantee you we can find a way."

"How?" Aly puckered, "I am absolutely not swimming that far in those cold, shark infested waters!"

And then came a voice as if from heaven, though standing right behind us:

"Would a canoe help?"

Chapter Fourteen

We all jumped and turned to see a kid of about ten standing behind us.

"I saw you running this way, and I ran behind you. The pastor is my hero, and I want to help. I have a canoe, if you want to use it you can."

"We do, young man, oh boy, do we ever!"

"Timothy, the name is Timothy."

"Thank you, Timothy. Now please, take us to that canoe as fast as you can."

He ran, and we bolted off behind him. That kid was fast! The pastor had obviously made an impact on him, for he was running like his own life depended on it.

"Wow," Aly puffed as she rushed to keep up, "this kid would make a good Night Hero!"

"Yes, he would," I puffed back. "But who knows what plans the Lord has for him. In the meantime, we just need to try and keep up!"

After twenty minutes or so we were back at the mouth of the Molasses Creek. A quick turn inland up an offshoot of it, and we skidded to a halt at a tiny shack by the shallow water.

"Here it is," he said as he uncovered it. He looked at it proudly, as if it were the finest sailing vessel on the water.

"It is a hollowed-out log," Carrie said with obvious concern.

"Yep, I made it myself," he said smiling. "Here are some paddles; let's go!"

"Whoa, Timothy, hold up for a second," I said as I put my hands on his shoulders. "We can't let you come; it is far too dangerous."

"I'm not afraid, not even a little," he said with the greatest determination I had ever seen.

"I believe you," I said as I smiled down at him. "But I still can't let you come. I need you to do some things for me here if this is going to work."

"What can I do? Just name it!"

"Good," I said, "very good. The first thing I need you to do is to go back into town and ring the church bell, and don't stop ringing it until everyone is there. Once everyone arrives, I need you to explain to them that my sisters and I are paddling over to that island to meet the enemy. Then I need you to get everyone to help us in the strongest way possible. Do you know what that is?"

"I sure do," he grinned, and without another word he was off like he had been shot out of a cannon.

"Good kid, that one," I said as I shook my head in amazement. It was always surprising to me the little things and little people God could use to do His biggest works.

"Kyle," Carrie said very slowly, "about this 'tree-canoe' and the open ocean..."

"Don't think about it, Sis, just paddle."

And we did, all of us.

Being out in the open water on an unbalanced, homemade canoe was maybe the most interesting thing we had ever done. In a kayak any of us could have done that mile in half an hour or less. But between trying desperately to not tip over, fighting leaks, and the weight of the log, it took us several hours to get ashore.

We intentionally picked the most wooded spot we could see and quickly got the canoe up out of the water and covered up by brush.

"Do you think they saw us?"

"I doubt it, Littlest Sis. For starters, they are not expecting anyone to have any way to follow or any courage to follow if they did have a way. Beyond that, though, that canoe has such a low profile in the water that it would take a miracle for anyone to see it unless they were right up on it.

Battery Island is tiny, just 103 acres, and it sits just across from Striking Island. This would be a potentially huge advantage for us. We could very likely circle the entire island in a matter of a few hours and should not have any trouble finding that wretched pirate ship.

That was the plan.

Which proved to be entirely unnecessary.

As if blown in by the very wind of Hades, at that very moment she rounded the edge of the island. And I kid you not, the weather came with her. In front of her had been the same dull grey skies of the morning. But as she came into view, a fog came with her, a devilish, thick, heavy fog.

We sat just back in the tree line, utterly still. We wanted to see them, but we did not want them to see us.

"What do we do, Kyle?"

"We wait, Carrie, we wait, and we do so very quietly," I whispered back.

"Why is it right here?"

"Why else?" I grinned. "We have a little honorary Night Hero back in town leading a prayer meeting for us."

And he was. The Conductor later told me that five minutes earlier little Timothy had stunned the entire town as he mounted the steps and calmly strode up behind the pulpit.

"Good people of Crosstown," he began in his most solemn ten-year-old voice...

He briefly explained what was happening, and immediately called everyone to prayer, which he himself then led:

"Our Father, we come before you this day as a needy people. But it is not for ourselves alone that we come, Lord, but also for your manservant, our good pastor, and for Mrs. Lydia. We come especially, though, for the three that you have sent to us to help in our hour of need.

"The psalmist said, Lord, that you inclined unto him and heard his cry. Incline unto us also, Lord, and hear our cry. Defend these that you have graciously sent to us, defend them, and give them success.

"They are seeking our enemies, Lord. I pray thee, make their task easy. Bring the enemy to them, Lord, right to where they are, and give them the victory on our behalf."

It was good that he was praying, because it didn't take us long to be reminded that this was indeed spiritual warfare we were facing.

"This fog, Kyle, it just isn't natural," Carrie said as she studied it with her eyes.

"I have to agree, Sis."

We quickly grabbed some small LED flashlights out of our bag, and they were needed. I tell you that mist, that fog, was supernatural. It was as if the devil himself were breathing it out to cover his precious pirates and their vile vessel.

It was so heavy that it was almost hard to breath. And with it came a feeling of oppression, as if the very forces of hell were all about us. We got very, very scared, and poured our hearts out to God for a very long time.

Finally, in the midst of the darkness, I could feel a peace come over me. No, the fog was not any less heavy, nor the task any easier, nor the oppression any lighter. But God has this way of giving peace within the midst of the darkest trial, and He was doing so for me now. Certainly not a giddy happiness, but a peace, a peace that passes all understanding.

The circumstances had not changed, though.

The heavy mist hung in the air like a shroud, blinding us to what we needed to see. I wondered if she was still there or had perhaps put silently out to sea for some reason. But the next breeze that blew reminded me how foolish that notion was. When the mist parted for briefest of times, there she was, black sails still hanging, the ghost ship that the people for miles around feared as if she was death itself.

"What now, Big Brother?" Carrie asked with a tinge of fear.

"We really don't have much of an option left to us, now do we?" I answered matter-of-factly. "I have to get aboard that ship."

Chapter Fifteen

"Rethink that choice of pronouns, Kyle," Aly snapped, "because YOU are not going aboard that ship; WE are going aboard that ship."

I grinned my biggest grin.

"Of course, we are, Aly, after all, I have to live with you two for the next few years. Okay, let's get our plan set."

After a quick discussion, we quietly slipped down to the canoe, uncovered it, and slid it stealthily into the water. It was kind of nice to realize that the very fog the devil had intended to use to hide his ship from us would also serve to hide ours from them.

One conundrum that we faced was the realization that at some point over the next few hours, we would need to bed down for our nightly trip home. But how would we do that if we were onboard a pirate ship doing battle? Hopefully our general plan would work, because that is about all we had to work with. It wasn't really possible to be too very specific until we were aboard and knew what we were dealing with.

We were pretty quickly right up beside the ship. I got us over to near the anchor chain, because that is how we planned on climbing aboard. Before we did, though, I took my knife out and spent about ten minutes using it to bore a hole in the canoe. I did not want it floating around and banging into the ship, alerting our enemies to our presence.

Once it started filling up with water, we slipped into the sea and quietly swam to the anchor chain. Climbing it would be no problem for any of us, our only question was what would we face once we got aboard?

The boom from a gun stunned us so badly we almost had heart attacks right there in the water!

"Avast, ye scurvy dogs," came a thundering voice from the deck. "Tis party time!"

The thunderous roar that quickly went up let me know that they were not kidding, but also that we were not even being thought about, much less suspected as being about to climb aboard.

The next hour was both miserable and encouraging. It was miserable in that we were stuck down in the water hanging onto the chain. But it was encouraging in that we could smell the evil odor of the rum flowing freely on deck.

"They are going to drink themselves into a stupor," Carrie said as she shivered and shook her head.

"Probably," I said, "but that is awfully good for us! Let's start climbing and see what there is to see."

We climbed quickly but quietly, and the noise from on deck was still steady, but much more slurred than before. These guys drank fast and hard, and the devil's brew that they were putting to their lips would be their downfall.

When we got to the top of the chain at the edge of the deck, I looked over and saw a jumbled mess. People were laying all over the place, some passed out, some diving deeply into their own personal bottle and about to pass out.

We noiselessly climbed aboard and started picking our way to the hatch on deck that Carrie was sure would lead to the lower levels, including the brig, where our folks were likely being held. I did not want to be seen, but sure enough, one half drunk yet still awake pirate rolled up onto one knee just as we passed. His eyes grew wide, and he opened his mouth to shout.

One hard right cross to his jaw prevented that shout from ever coming. He would get his best night's sleep ever but would not be able to chew solid food for months.

We quickly rushed to the hatch, opened it up, and slid down inside it, closing it behind us. Down the ladder, into the hold, LED lights clicked on, and we began a frantic search.

"Kyle, over here!" Aly hissed.

Carrie and I converged on her, and sure enough, we found our missing people. There, in a corner of a cell was the pastor, and he looked to have been beaten badly. On the other side of him was Lydia, trying to tend to his wounds.

They looked up and saw us, and seemed utterly stunned, then they began to cry.

"Oh, dear children," the pastor moaned, "Have you been taken also? May the heavens be merciful, and may God deliver us from such evil!"

"He is merciful, Pastor, and delivery is exactly why we are here. We have not been taken, we have come. We are here to rescue you, both of you."

Carrie and Aly started to scurry about and look for a key to unlock the huge padlock that held the door shut. The pastor shut his eyes, and I could not tell if he was resting or had passed out.

"How is the pastor?" I asked Lydia.

"Bless him," she cooed, "He has been braver than David and stronger than Samson. Each time anyone has come for us, he has stood in the way and fought with them. The pirates seem to think it great sport, but I tell you, he has held his own remarkably well. So well that since he has been here, none has touched me."

"Backbone like a saw log, just as I suspected" I grinned.

"Kyle, we can't find a key anywhere!"

"And you won't," Lydia moaned. "The captain keeps it with him at all times, it is never out of his possession unless he sends someone down here to open or close the cell doors.

"That is a problem," I said, "but not one that is insurmountable, as long as we use the strongest muscle we have. Carrie, find me something like a towel, Aly find me a stick."

In short order they had brought me both, Carrie had produced a feed sack of sorts, and Aly some type of a mop handle.

"Young man," the pastor moaned as he opened his eyes, "I have no idea what you are planning, but it would take a miracle of God for you to open a lock with fabric and a stick. Nonetheless, I do thank you for coming, your bravery and sacrifice are commendable indeed."

"Bravery, maybe, Pastor, but I do not intend on the sacrifice part if it can be avoided, not for any of us. As for the miracle, yes, but perhaps not the kind you think. This will be a miracle of, as a man of both science and faith named Newton once said, 'Thinking God's thoughts after him.'

"God has built laws into His creation, and sometimes He uses the most unlikely of sources to teach us those laws and their practical applications. At our home church we once had a man who had gotten saved out of a criminal life. He taught this leverage trick to my father, for good purposes."

While I was speaking, I had taken the cloth, cut a nice wide strip out of it, and looped it through the lock. I tied it firmly together, and then looped the stick through it. Then I started twisting the stick. The cloth pulled tight, and as I continued to twist, "Pop!" The lock came loose.

We quickly opened the door and started back up the ladder. My plan at this point was to find the small boat that the pirates had been using to come ashore and get it and all of us out into the water.

But somehow, the point of a sword has a way of changing plans.

"Hello there, young mateys," the captain leered as he stared down at us through the hatch, "and welcome aboard the Ghost Ship."

Then he laughed, a slurred, evil, drunken, frightening laugh.

Chapter Sixteen

As we stood on deck surrounded by pirate's swords and pistols, the captain was clearly in rare form and enjoying the moment.

"It reminds me of the Incredibles," Aly whispered, "where Syndrome is 'monologuing.'"

It did, actually. He was going on at length about his power and prowess, "king of the high seas," on ad nauseam. He was an ugly man, with a huge scar all the way across his face from some previous slash from a cutlass.

"What now, guys?" I asked in whisper while the captain continued to extol his greatness.

"I have an idea," Carrie said, "but you probably aren't going to like it."

"Spit it out, Sis, it can't be much more dangerous than anything I've faced before. If I can deal with the blade of Black Crow, I can probably handle whatever idea you have for me to deal with this jerk."

"That's awfully nice of you, Brother," she said with a tinge of sarcasm in her voice, "but, sadly, not everything is actually about you. This is, in fact, about what God will hopefully do with and through me."

Now that one caught me off guard, I had to admit.

"What do you mean, Carrie?"

"It all fits together, Kyle, it really does. What was it that you pointed out to the townsfolk about pirates in general, and this one in particular?"

"Pride. This man is eaten up with it. Just look at him, he is giving himself the Nobel Prize for piracy as we speak."

He really was. I will not bore you with the details, but he was staggering across the deck almost in a pirouette, pontificating on his perceived greatness, bragging like a fool from the book of Proverbs.

"So, he is eaten up with pride," I said. "What does that have to do with you?"

"Lots. Tell me, of the three of us, which one has picked up the quickest on the lessons dad has given us with the wooden karate swords?"

"Um, Sis, we all know that the answer is you, but I don't think I like where this is headed."

"Relax, Kyle, I don't intend to get into a long drawn out fencing match, nor do I think I could handle him under normal circumstances. But these are not normal circumstances, mostly since old Captain Hook there is so drunk he is having trouble standing up. My intention is to goad him into an embarrassing fight, and in so doing have every eye on us. Who in the world would be looking elsewhere while a girl holds her own with a pirate captain in a sword fight?

"In the meantime, I assume you have your pocketknife handy?"

I just gave her my special glare that means *Now what do you think?*

"Good," she said. "While I have everyone's attention, cut yourself loose, hand the knife to the others and have them do the same while you start the fire."

"Um, what? Fire?"

"Yes, Kyle, fire. It isn't like pirates have auto insurance on their ships. Lose the ship, and you are out of the piracy business. Furthermore, history tells us that most of these bozos can't even swim."

"But what about us and the ones we came to rescue?"

In answer to that, she nodded upward and to the left with her head. As I turned, I smiled, for hanging there by the edge of the second level was the very boat we had been hoping to find and use.

"Are you sure about this?"

"Kyle, trust me; it will be my pleasure."

Apparently so, because when she went to work, it was a thing of beauty.

"BAHAHAHAHAHAHA! What a load of hooey!" she shouted. The effect was instantaneous. Everything on deck fell silent, and the captain went white with rage.

"What did ye say?"

"You heard me, you worthless landlubber posing as a pirate. Great? You aren't great. You are a tiny, weak, cowardly man unfit to lead. Why, any man here would make a better captain than you, and any girl here would make a better swordsman than you, especially me."

Every eye on deck was as wide as a platter at that moment, and every jaw was hanging wide open. Carrie pushed her advantage:

"You handle that blade as gracefully as a mule eating briars. I could take any blade here and spank you with it, and I would gladly do so if you would be so kind as to untie my hands. Or, are you afraid, little man, afraid that a little girl will embarrass you in front of your men?"

The captain was stunned, but also in a real bind. The only thing worse than responding to the taunts of a girl would be not responding. But Carrie was not done, not quite yet.

"I am not Anne Bonny, you coward. If I were her, I know for certain you would not want to tangle with me. I am just a little girl named Carrie. You would cry if Anne Bonny called you out, are you going to cry in front of your men now that I have done so?"

Oh my, that was good, that was really good! My sister's memory of what she had read in those two pirate books was really paying some rich dividends right now. Anne Bonny was a famous woman pirate. But, men being what they were in those days, every male captain positively chafed at the mere mention of her name. To have her name invoked in front of these men would be like waving a red cape in front of a bull. He would take her up on her challenge, he would not have any choice.

The captain grew coldly, furiously angry, he was absolutely trembling with rage. He pointed his sword and walked straight toward Carrie. I was as tense as a violin string, ready to jump in between them.

"Swish!"

Suddenly Carrie was standing with her cords cut, her hands free. That was scary; drunk or not that was a very quick and precise movement.

"Give the lass a sword, boatswain," the captain said coldly.

Carrie moved to the very front of the deck, drawing all eyes with her as the boatswain brought her a blade. Furiously, I fished my knife out of my pocket and cut through the ropes holding my hands together. Then I handed the knife to Aly and disappeared behind the wheelhouse.

Chapter Seventeen

Hey, this is Carrie, I will pick it up from here. As the boatswain was handing me the sword, out of the corner of my eye I saw Kyle disappear from view. "Five minutes," I told myself, "just give him five minutes and that will be enough."

I looked the sword over and swung it around a few times to get the feel of it and to kill some time. It was the same length as the wooden sword dad had taught me to use so well, but considerably heavier. I would have to take that into account with every movement. Hopefully, his drunken state would slow him down enough to even things up.

The captain stood about five foot eight, pretty standard for a man in those days. I am five foot five, not too big of a difference, which was good. He weighed maybe thirty pounds more than me, but that really did not matter much. A blade cuts just as well no matter a person's weight.

"Are ye ready fer yer beatin, little miss loudmouth?"

Words would not be nearly as good of an answer at that moment as a visual answer.

Swinging the sword from my left side to up behind my right shoulder, I stepped back smoothly with my right foot, left elbow down, right fist and sword pointed straight ahead. Every jaw on deck dropped again. Dad would have been proud, I think.

The captain shook his head in disbelief, then began to circle, his sword held in his right hand alone, his left hand out in front of him along with it. That was good, very good. It told me that this man actually knew very little about swordplay and had gotten by with his men mostly on threats and bluster. I was absolutely going to enjoy this!

I stepped across with my right, shifting the sword to my left shoulder, and then back again as I stepped another step with my left.

Suddenly he lunged, and I easily swung my sword in a quick circle over my head and down, knocking this thrust aside easily, then doing a full spin to arrive back in a defensive position once again, just as I had started.

The gasp from the assemblage on deck was audible. I knew for certain that every eye was on me. Kyle could be standing on his head on top of the mast gargling peanut butter and no one would have noticed.

The captain shook his head again as if to get his thoughts together. Clearly this is not what he had expected. As quickly as he could he dropped his blade downward, swung it in a full circle overhead, and brought it down toward my head, clearly trying to split my head in half. There is no way I could block that kind of force, but there was also no need for me to do so.

I spun completely to the left by turning completely clockwise and sidestepping. At the same time, I turned my blade flat side and swung for the fences, like I was trying to smash a baseball. The flat of my blade went "Thwack!" against his bent over backside, and he went sprawling out on the deck, howling in pain and anger.

He quickly jumped up to face me again, and I smirked at him. "I told you I would spank you with it; did you not believe me?"

I guess my brother is luckier than me. With Black Crow, his anger had gotten the better of him and he had gotten careless. This guy was mean, foolish, and drunk, but not careless, at least not yet. He clearly knew that he was not in prime condition in his drunken state and that I was more of a danger that he had suspected.

Much more carefully, he began to take tiny stabbing lunges at me. Each time I easily swatted his blade away. This was good, no, excellent, really. It was providing Kyle with valuable time. I just hoped it would be enough.

Chapter Eighteen

This is Kyle again, I will take it from here. While Carrie was on deck, I was below deck working furiously and worrying profusely. I had piled every flammable thing I could quickly lay my hands on in a pile underneath a low deck. Feed sacks, cloth, food, kegs of rum, everything.

Once I had what I believed to be a sufficient amount for an unstoppable blaze, I ripped a lantern from the wall and smashed it onto the floor right at the foot of my pile of fuel. Instantly it burst into a blaze and started to climb the very walls of the ship. There was no going back now, and there was no way anyone could put out that blaze.

I raced to the other side of the hold and came back up on deck on the other side. It would not take more than a couple of minutes for the ship to be engulfed in flames.

I looked to the front of the ship, and everyone was still gathered in a wide circle around Carrie and the Captain. Good heavens, she was absolutely giving him fits! She was a step quicker with each move, as graceful as a ballet dancer, and as precise as a surgeon.

I rushed to the landing boat and lowered it into the water. The pastor and Lydia saw me at that very moment. Aly shoved them toward me, and I got them overboard and into the boat.

It was then that the flames burst through the lower hold and onto the deck. It climbed the main sail like lightning, and suddenly every eye turned toward it.

"It's over, dirt bag," I shouted. "You are now a pirate without a vessel to command. And, as you have been thoroughly bested by a mere girl in a duel of swords, I suspect that you have no men to command either."

His eyes grew wide, and a look of demonic fury seized him. In uncontrolled wrath, knowing he was done, he turned and rushed at Carrie, blade leveled throat high.

"NOOO!" I screamed helplessly, knowing I could never get there in time.

Hey, this is Carrie again. When I saw the captain rush at me, I instantly knew my options were limited. I was on the very point of the deck, so behind me and to each side was overboard and the cold water. Ahead of me was the maniac of the high seas rushing toward me. There was literally nowhere good to go, I could not believe I had so carelessly allowed myself into this position as badly as I had beaten him up until now.

It's sort of funny, really, how quickly things go through your mind. All during my sword duel with the drunken captain, in the back of my mind I had been thinking about the last few verses of Proverbs 23, which ironically enough talk about a drunk guy on a ship, and how much damage he does to himself. But it was another verse from Proverbs that saved me now, specifically Proverbs 26:27 which says "Whoso diggeth a pit shall fall therein: and he that rolleth a stone, it will return upon him." It basically means that people try to destroy others but are destroyed by their own plans and devices. That immediately brought a follow up thought to me:

"Use their own force against them," I could hear my dad saying as he trained us.

A split second before the blade would have run me through, I dropped to my hands and knees. The captain ran right into me as the blade went over top of me, and instantly I pushed back up onto my feet, screaming for extra power.

The last sight anyone ever had of this unholy terror was of him flying overboard and into the dark waters.

The crew stood, stunned, unsure of what to do. I raced to the landing boat, dove into it, and we shoved off. Kyle and the pastor rowed like madmen, and the rest of us watched as the men on the ship dove off of the boat into the water. They were near enough to shore that they would all likely make it. They would be helpless and stranded, but I doubted if anyone in the area would ever complain about that.

"What should we do with them now, young man? You have organized and performed all of this, what do you recommend?"

Kyle smiled and said, "Pastor, send word to the governor of Virginia. He is a good man and would love the opportunity to pick up a bunch of wicked fish in a barrel like this. I would suspect that even if they are ever pardoned and released, none of them will ever want anything to do with Crosstown again."

My brother looked over at me in wonder and smiled. "Sis," he said, "remind me never to make you angry, especially if there is a sword anywhere nearby."

"Bro," I smiled back, "trust me. Even if there is no sword anywhere nearby, you better have enough sense never to make me angry."

Kyle shook his head and grinned, and everyone else in the boat broke out into a healthy fit of relieved laughter. Me, I grinned in relief and silently thanked God for giving me strength beyond my strength. Pirates? Yeah, with God, we got this...

Epilog and Historical Information

Edward Low was a real pirate, and the description of him in this book is based on historical information. Following is a section from the book *Pirates of Colonial North Carolina* by Hugh F. Rankin:

"Captain Edward Low's 'Fancy' captured a number of prizes in the waters off North Carolina. His black flag, with red skeleton outlined on it, struck terror into the hearts of many an honest seaman. He was feared more than the general run of pirates because it was reported, and believed, the man was insane. He was described by writers of the period as being a 'ferocious brute,'" and noted for cruelty to prisoners...

"His quick temper resulted in many mutilations among his captives. Perhaps this can best be explained by his own ugly face, which had been severely slashed with a cutlass. Because of an argument with his surgeon, Low had tried to sew the wound himself, making a horrible botch of the job. From this time on, his misshapen face only added to the terror of his reputation...

"He would rip the masts out of a captured vessel and then set its crew adrift in the trackless waste of the sea. And upon some occasions, he was even reported to have chained a crew aboard its vessel before setting it afire. Low was never captured, and no one knows how he met his end. He simply disappeared."

Coming Soon

When Serpents Rise

The power of prejudice was as subtle and persuasive as ever, and apparently I was living proof of that. But now that I knew better, could this disaster be stopped? I looked out the window of the tiny cabin up on the hill and could see movement in the trees down below. The Pit Viper and his posse were headed this way, and if history was a good indicator, they would not be taking any prisoners, including us. From the back of the room I could hear Rain Water moaning. He was in no shape to fight and no shape to run.

"We have company coming, Guys," I said to Carrie and Aly, "and I don't think they're bringing house warming gifts."

If we were lucky, this would be a very long day. If we were not, we may not live long enough to see tomorrow.

Other Books in the Night Heroes Series

Cry From the Coal Mine

Free Fall

Broken Brotherhood

The Blade of Black Crow

Other Books by Dr. Wagner

From Footers to Finish Nails

Beyond the Colored Coat

Daniel: Breathtaking

Esther: Five Feasts and the Fingerprints of God

Nehemiah: A Labor of Love

Marriage Makers/Marriage Breakers

I'm Saved! Now What???

Don't Muzzle the Ox

www.ingramcontent.com/pod-product-compliance
Lightning Source LLC
Chambersburg PA
CBHW071925220626
47052CB00002B/457

* 9 7 8 1 9 4 1 0 3 9 9 7 7 *